Apple Tree
Station

Apple Tree
Village

Church

School

Manor

The Runaway Tractor

Heather Amery

Adapted by Anna Milbourne

Illustrated by Stephen Cartwright

Reading consultant: Alison Kelly

This story is about
Apple Tree Farm,

Sam,

Poppy,

Ted,

Farmer Dray,

Dolly

and a
tractor.

One day, Poppy and
Sam were raking leaves.

The tractor chugged
past.

Ted was taking some
hay to the sheep.

The children went to play in the barn. Then Sam heard a shout.

What's that?

They ran outside.

The tractor was out
of control.

The trailer came off...

Crash!

and the tractor landed
in the pond.

Splash!

Poppy and Sam ran.

"I'm all wet," said Ted.

"How can we get the
tractor out?" he asked.

Poppy and Sam soon came back.

Farmer Dray had his horse, Dolly.

Ted tied ropes
to the tractor.

Farmer Dray tied them to Dolly's harness.

Ted pushed.

Go on, Dolly!

Dolly pulled.

The tractor began
to move.

The tractor came out
of the water.

Ted fell in.

"So do I!" said Ted.

Poppy and Sam had a
ride home on Dolly.

Poor Ted had to walk.

Puzzles

Puzzle 1

Put these pictures in the right order to tell the story.

A.

B.

C.

D.

E.

23

Puzzle 2

Who's who? Match the names to the people or animals in this story.

Ted

Poppy

Dolly

Farmer Dray

Sam

Puzzle 3

Can you spot five differences between these two pictures?

Puzzle 4

Which sentence goes with each picture?

A.

They saw a noise.

They heard a noise.

B.

"I'm all wet," said Ted.

"I'm not wet," said Ted.

C.

Dolly pulled.
Dolly pushed.

D.

Poor Ted had to talk.
Poor Ted had to walk.

Answers to puzzles
Puzzle 1

1C.

2E.

3D.

4A.

5B.

Puzzle 2

Dolly

Farmer Dray

Poppy

Ted

Sam

Puzzle 3

Puzzle 4

A.
They heard
a noise.

B.
"I'm all wet,"
said Ted.

C.
Dolly
pulled.

D.
Poor Ted had
to walk.

Designed by Laura Nelson
Series editor: Lesley Sims
Series designer: Russell Punter
Digital manipulation by Nick Wakeford

This edition first published in 2015 by Usborne Publishing Ltd.,
Usborne House, 83-85 Saffron Hill, London EC1N 8RT, England.
www.usborne.com Copyright © 2015, 1989 Usborne Publishing Ltd.

USBORNE FIRST READING
Level Two

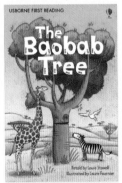